D0832865

MINI CLASSICS

THE

HAPPY
PRINCE

A PARRAGON BOOK

Published by
Parragon Books,
Unit 13-17, Avonbridge Trading Estate,
Atlantic Road, Avonmouth, Bristol BS11 9QD.

Produced by
The Templar Company plc,
Pippbrook Mill, London Road, Dorking, Surrey RH4 1JE.

Copyright © 1994 Parragon Book Service Limited

Designed by Mark Kingsley-Monks

Printed and bound in Great Britain

ISBN 1-85813-605-9

MINI CLASSICS

THE

HAPPY PRINCE

RETOLD BY STEPHANIE LASLETT
ILLUSTRATED BY SUSAN NEALE

||| ·PARRAGON· |||

High above the city on a tall column stood the statue of the Happy Prince. He was gilded all over with thin leaves of fine gold, for eyes he had two bright sapphires and a large red ruby glowed on his sword-hilt.

The city people were very proud of their fine statue.

"Why can't you be like the Happy Prince?" asked a sensible mother when she found her little boy crying for the moon. "The Happy Prince never dreams of crying for anything."

"I am glad to see there is someone in the world who is quite happy," muttered a disappointed man as he gazed at the wonderful statue.

"He looks just like an angel," said the Charity Children as they came out of the cathedral in their bright scarlet cloaks and

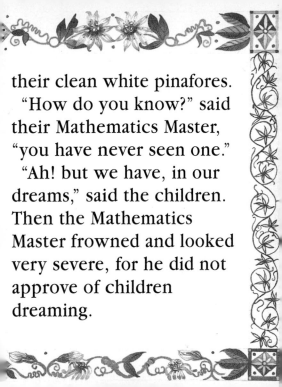

their clean white pinafores.
"How do you know?" said
their Mathematics Master,
"you have never seen one."
"Ah! but we have, in our
dreams," said the children.
Then the Mathematics
Master frowned and looked
very severe, for he did not
approve of children
dreaming.

Far away from the city lived a little Swallow. His friends had gone away to Egypt six weeks before, but he had stayed behind, for he was in love with the most beautiful Reed.

He had met her early in the spring as he was flying down the river after a big yellow moth, and he had been so attracted by her slender waist that he had stopped to talk to her.

"Shall I love you?" said the
Swallow, who liked to come
to the point at once, and the
Reed made him a low bow
in reply. So he flew happily
round and round her,
touching the water with
his wings, and making
silver ripples. This was his
courtship, and it lasted all
through the summer.

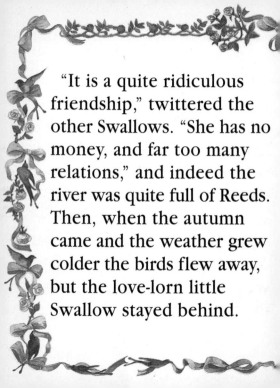

"It is a quite ridiculous friendship," twittered the other Swallows. "She has no money, and far too many relations," and indeed the river was quite full of Reeds. Then, when the autumn came and the weather grew colder the birds flew away, but the love-lorn little Swallow stayed behind.

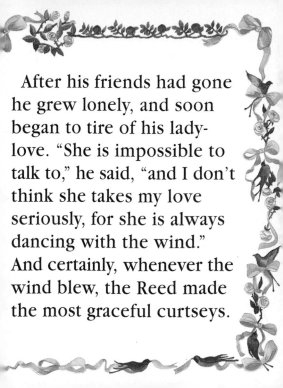

After his friends had gone he grew lonely, and soon began to tire of his lady-love. "She is impossible to talk to," he said, "and I don't think she takes my love seriously, for she is always dancing with the wind." And certainly, whenever the wind blew, the Reed made the most graceful curtseys.

"Will you come away with
me?" he said to her finally,
but the Reed shook her
head. She was too fond of
her home.

"You have been trifling
with me," he cried. "I am
off to the Pyramids in
Egypt. Good-bye!" and
away he flew.

All day long he flew, and

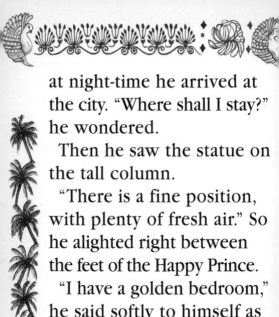

at night-time he arrived at
the city. "Where shall I stay?"
he wondered.

Then he saw the statue on
the tall column.

"There is a fine position,
with plenty of fresh air." So
he alighted right between
the feet of the Happy Prince.

"I have a golden bedroom,"
he said softly to himself as

he prepared to go to sleep, but just as he put his head under his wing a large drop of water fell on him.

"What a curious thing!" he cried. "There is not a single cloud in the sky, the stars are quite clear and bright, and yet it is raining. The climate in the north of Europe is really dreadful."

Then another drop fell.
"What is the use of a statue
if it cannot keep the rain
off?" he said. "I must look for
a good chimney-pot," and
he got ready to fly away.

But before he had opened his wings, a third drop fell. He looked up and saw — ah! what did he see?

The eyes of the Happy Prince were filled with tears, and tears were running down his golden cheeks. His face was so beautiful in the moonlight that the little Swallow was filled with pity.

"Who are you?" he said.

"I am the Happy Prince," replied the statue.

"But why are you crying?" asked the Swallow. "You have quite drenched me."

"When I was alive and had a human heart," answered the statue, "I did not know what tears were, for I lived in the Palace of Sans-Souci,

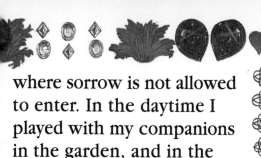

where sorrow is not allowed
to enter. In the daytime I
played with my companions
in the garden, and in the
evening I danced in the
Great Hall. All around the
garden ran a very high wall,
but I never once wondered
what lay beyond it, because
everything about me was
so beautiful. My courtiers

called me the Happy Prince, and happy indeed I was, if pleasure be happiness. So I lived, and so I died. And now that I am dead they have set me up here so high that I can see all the ugliness and all the misery of my city, and though my heart is made of lead yet I cannot help but weep.

"Far away in a little street there is a poor house," continued the statue in a low musical voice. "One of the windows is open, and through it I can see a woman seated at a table."

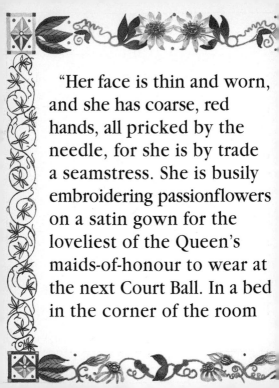

"Her face is thin and worn, and she has coarse, red hands, all pricked by the needle, for she is by trade a seamstress. She is busily embroidering passionflowers on a satin gown for the loveliest of the Queen's maids-of-honour to wear at the next Court Ball. In a bed in the corner of the room

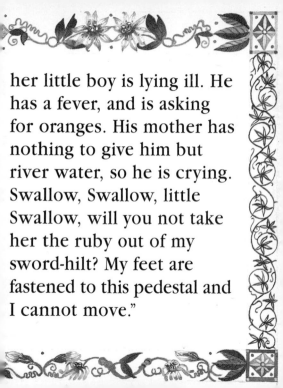

her little boy is lying ill. He has a fever, and is asking for oranges. His mother has nothing to give him but river water, so he is crying. Swallow, Swallow, little Swallow, will you not take her the ruby out of my sword-hilt? My feet are fastened to this pedestal and I cannot move."

"My friends are waiting for me in Egypt," said the little Swallow. "They are flying up and down the River Nile over the large lotus-flowers. Soon they will go to sleep

in the tomb of the great
King. There he lies in his
painted coffin. He is wrapped
in soft yellow linen, and
embalmed with spices.
Round his neck is a chain

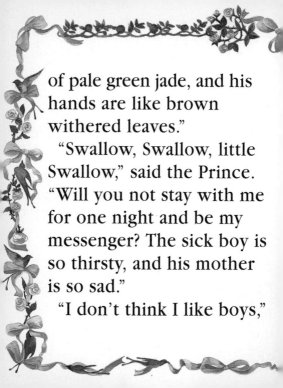

of pale green jade, and his hands are like brown withered leaves."

"Swallow, Swallow, little Swallow," said the Prince. "Will you not stay with me for one night and be my messenger? The sick boy is so thirsty, and his mother is so sad."

"I don't think I like boys,"

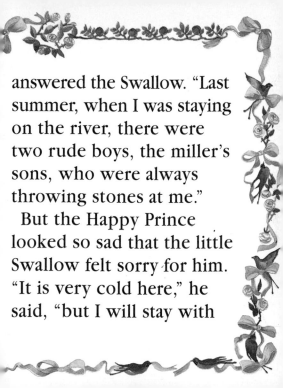

answered the Swallow. "Last summer, when I was staying on the river, there were two rude boys, the miller's sons, who were always throwing stones at me."

But the Happy Prince looked so sad that the little Swallow felt sorry for him. "It is very cold here," he said, "but I will stay with

you for one night, and be
your messenger."

"Thank you, little Swallow,"
said the Prince.

So the Swallow picked out
the great ruby from the
Prince's sword, and flew
away with it in his beak
over the roofs of the town.
He passed by the cathedral's
white marble angels.

He passed by the Palace and heard the sound of dancing. A beautiful girl came out on the balcony with her lover.

"How wonderful the stars are tonight," he said to her, "and how wonderful is the power of love!"

"I hope my dress will be ready in time for the State Ball," she answered. "I have ordered passionflowers to be embroidered on it, but the seamstresses are so lazy."

He passed over the river, and at last he came to the poor house and looked in at the window. The boy tossed feverishly on his bed.

His mother was so tired that she had fallen asleep. The little Swallow hopped through the window and laid the great ruby on the table beside the woman's thimble. Then he flew round the bed, gently fanning the boy's forehead with his wings.

"How cool I feel!" said

the boy. "I must be getting better," and he sank into a delicious slumber.

Then the Swallow flew back to the Happy Prince, and told him what he had done. "It is curious," the little bird remarked, "but I feel quite warm now, even though the night is so bitterly cold."

"That is because you have done a good deed," said the Happy Prince. Then the little Swallow began to think, but soon he fell fast asleep. Thinking always made him sleepy.

When day broke he flew down to the river and had a bath. "What a remarkable phenomenon!" said the

Professor of Ornithology (which, as I am sure you already know, is the study of birds) as he was passing over the bridge. "A swallow in winter!"

"To-night I fly to Egypt," said the Swallow happily. He flew all over the city and wherever he went the Sparrows chirruped, and

said to each other, "Look!
There is a swallow. What a
distinguished stranger!" so
he enjoyed himself greatly.
When the moon rose he
flew to the Happy Prince.

"Is there anything you want me to bring back from Egypt?" he cried. "I am just leaving."

"Swallow, Swallow, little Swallow," said the Prince. "Will you not stay with me one night longer?"

"They are waiting for me in Egypt," answered the Swallow. "Tomorrow my friends will fly up the River Nile to the great waterfall. At noon the yellow lions come down to the water's edge to drink. They have eyes like green beryl jewels, and their roar is louder than the roar of the waterfall."

"Swallow, Swallow, little Swallow," said the Prince. "Far away across the city I see a young man in a cramped attic. He is leaning over a desk covered with papers, and in a glass by his side there is a bunch of withered violets. His hair is brown and shiny and his lips are red as a pomegranate."

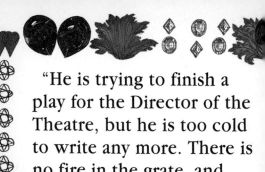

"He is trying to finish a play for the Director of the Theatre, but he is too cold to write any more. There is no fire in the grate, and hunger has made him feel weak and faint."

"I will wait with you one night longer," said the kind Swallow. "Shall I take him another ruby?"

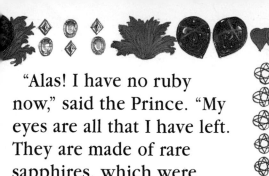

"Alas! I have no ruby now," said the Prince. "My eyes are all that I have left. They are made of rare sapphires, which were brought here from India a thousand years ago. Pluck one out and take it to him. He can then sell it to the jeweller and buy firewood and finish his play."

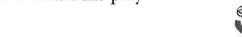

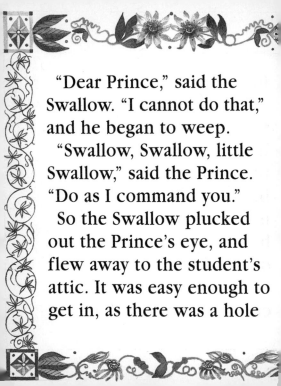

"Dear Prince," said the Swallow. "I cannot do that," and he began to weep.

"Swallow, Swallow, little Swallow," said the Prince. "Do as I command you."

So the Swallow plucked out the Prince's eye, and flew away to the student's attic. It was easy enough to get in, as there was a hole

in the roof.

There was the young man with his head buried in his hands. He did not hear the flutter of the bird's wings, but later when he looked up he found the beautiful blue sapphire lying on top of the withered violets.

"Appreciation at last," he cried gladly.

"This must be from some great admirer. Someone believes in me after all and now I can finish my play," and the young man happily rubbed his hands.

The next day the Swallow flew down to the harbour. He watched the sailors hauling big chests out of the hold with strong ropes. "Heave a-hoy!" they called as each chest came up.

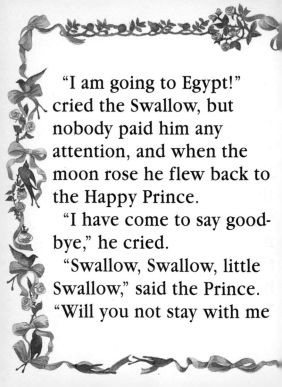

"I am going to Egypt!" cried the Swallow, but nobody paid him any attention, and when the moon rose he flew back to the Happy Prince.

"I have come to say good-bye," he cried.

"Swallow, Swallow, little Swallow," said the Prince. "Will you not stay with me

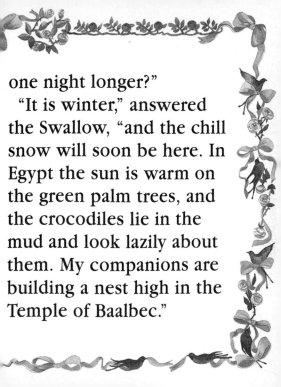

one night longer?"

"It is winter," answered the Swallow, "and the chill snow will soon be here. In Egypt the sun is warm on the green palm trees, and the crocodiles lie in the mud and look lazily about them. My companions are building a nest high in the Temple of Baalbec."

"There the pink and white doves are watching them, and cooing to each other. Dear Prince, I must leave you, but I will never forget you, and next spring I will bring you two beautiful jewels. The ruby shall be redder than a red rose, and the sapphire shall be as blue as the great sea."

"In the square below," said the Happy Prince, "there stands a little match-girl. She has let her matches fall in the gutter, and they are all spoiled. Her father will beat her if she does not bring home some money, and she is crying. She has no shoes or stockings, and her little head is bare. Pluck

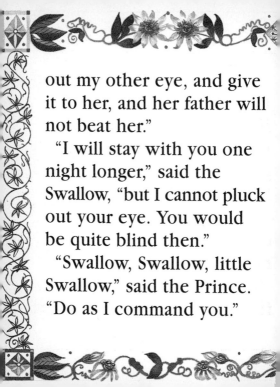

out my other eye, and give
it to her, and her father will
not beat her."

"I will stay with you one
night longer," said the
Swallow, "but I cannot pluck
out your eye. You would
be quite blind then."

"Swallow, Swallow, little
Swallow," said the Prince.
"Do as I command you."

So he plucked out the
Prince's other eye, and
flew down through the air.
He swooped past the match-
girl, and slipped the jewel
into the palm of her hand.

"What a lovely bit of glass!"
cried the little girl and she
ran home, laughing.

Then the Swallow slowly
flew back to the Prince.

"You are blind now," he said, "so I will stay with you always."

"No, little Swallow," said the poor Prince. "You must go away to Egypt."

"I will stay with you always," said the Swallow, and he slept at the Prince's golden feet.

All the next day he sat on

the Prince's shoulder, and
told him stories of what he
had seen in strange lands.
He told him of the red birds,
who stand in long rows on
the banks of the Nile and
catch goldfish in their
beaks. He told him of the
Sphinx, who is as old as
the world itself and lives in
the desert and knows

everything. He told him of
the merchants, who walk
slowly by the side of their
camels and carry amber
beads in their hands. He
told him of the King of the
Mountains of the Moon,
who is as black as ebony
and worships a large crystal.
He told him of the great
green snake that sleeps in a

palm tree and has twenty
priests to feed it with
honey-cakes; and of the
pygmies who sail over a
big lake on large flat leaves,
and are always at war with
the butterflies.

"Dear little Swallow," said
the Prince, "you tell me of
marvellous things, but what
of the suffering of people?

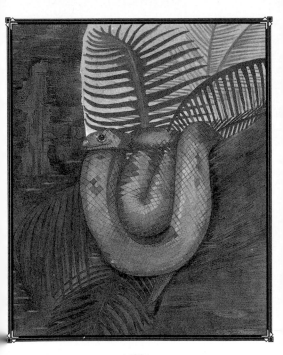

There is no Mystery so great as Misery. Fly over my city, little Swallow, and tell me what you see there."

So the Swallow flew over
the great city, and saw the
rich making merry in their
beautiful houses, while the
beggars were sitting at the
gates. He flew into dark
lanes, and saw the white

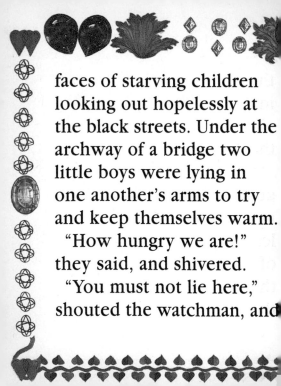

faces of starving children looking out hopelessly at the black streets. Under the archway of a bridge two little boys were lying in one another's arms to try and keep themselves warm.

"How hungry we are!" they said, and shivered.

"You must not lie here," shouted the watchman, and

the small boys wandered out into the rain and the dark.

Then he flew back and told the Prince what he had seen.

"I am covered with fine gold," said the Prince. "You must take if off, leaf by leaf, and give it to the poor of my city. People always think that gold can make them happy."

So the Swallow picked off leaf after leaf of the fine gold, till the Happy Prince looked quite dull and grey. Leaf after leaf of the fine gold he brought to the poor, and the children's faces grew rosier, and they laughed and played games in the street. "We have bread now!" they cried.

Then the snow came, and after the snow came the frost. The streets looked as if they were made of silver, and long icicles like crystal daggers hung down from the eaves of the houses.

Everybody went about in furs but the poor little Swallow grew colder and colder. Now he would not leave the Prince for he loved him too well. He picked up crumbs outside the baker's door when the baker was not looking, and tried to keep himself warm by flapping his wings.

But at last he knew that he was going to die. He had just enough strength to fly up to the Prince's shoulder once more. "Good-bye, dear Prince!" he murmured. "Will you let me kiss your hand before I leave?"

"I am glad that you are going to Egypt at last, little Swallow," said the Prince.

"You have stayed too long here, but you must kiss me on the lips, for I love you."

"It is not to Egypt that I am going," said the Swallow. "I am going to the House of Death. Death is the brother of Sleep, is he not?"

And he kissed the Happy Prince on the lips, and fell down dead at his feet.

At that moment a curious crack sounded inside the statue, as if something had broken. The fact is that the leaden heart had snapped right in two. It certainly was a dreadfully hard frost.

Early the next morning the Mayor and the Town Councillors were walking in the square below.

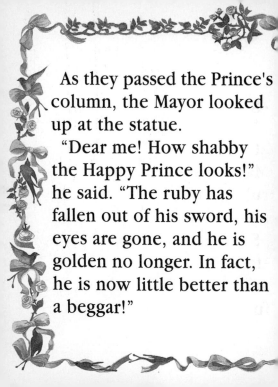

As they passed the Prince's column, the Mayor looked up at the statue.

"Dear me! How shabby the Happy Prince looks!" he said. "The ruby has fallen out of his sword, his eyes are gone, and he is golden no longer. In fact, he is now little better than a beggar!"

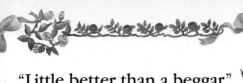

"Little better than a beggar," agreed all the Councillors.

"And here is a dead bird at his feet!" continued the Mayor. "We must issue a ruling that birds are not allowed to die here."

So they pulled down the statue of the Happy Prince and carried him off to the furnace to be melted. Then

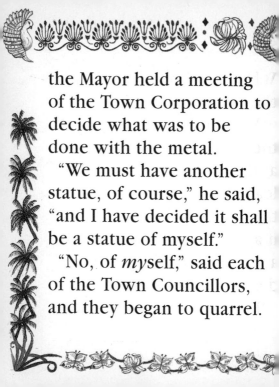

the Mayor held a meeting
of the Town Corporation to
decide what was to be
done with the metal.

"We must have another
statue, of course," he said,
"and I have decided it shall
be a statue of myself."

"No, of *myself*," said each
of the Town Councillors,
and they began to quarrel.

When I last heard of them they were quarrelling still.

"What a strange thing!" said the foreman of the workmen at the foundry. "This broken lead heart will not melt in the furnace. We must throw it away." So they threw it on a rubbish heap where the dead Swallow also lay.

"Bring Me the two most

precious things in the
city," said God to one of
His Angels and the Angel
brought Him the leaden
heart and the dead bird.

"You have chosen wisely,"
said God, "for in My garden
of Paradise this little bird
shall sing for evermore, and
in My city of gold the Happy
Prince shall praise Me."

OSCAR WILDE

Oscar Wilde (1854-1900) wrote
several fairy stories but was better
known for his poetry and plays.
The Happy Prince was published in
1888 and in common with his
other tales, such as *The Selfish Giant*,
shows the influence of Hans Christian
Andersen in its rather wistful
outlook on life.
Oscar Wilde read the stories to his
own children but declared that they
were intended for "childlike people
from eighteen to eighty".